RIPE TOMATOES

Ripe Tomatoes

a novella

Nora Ruth Roberts

Ripe Tomatoes
a novella
by Nora Ruth Roberts

ISBN 1-887128-39-5

Editorial Work on Ripe Tomatoes by
Sander Hicks, Cat Tyc, Varrick and Karla Zounek.

Front Cover Typography by Yankl Salant
Cover Art by the late, great Geo Smith.

We love you, Geo.

Soft Skull Press
100 Suffolk Street, NYC
www.softskull.com

The following is a work of fiction.

Any resemblance to any person living or dead is purely coincidental.

For Evelyn and for Alice

1

The theory that laid the groundwork for the Utopian tomato commune that started all this off was developed by the pre-Marxist socialists of the nineteenth century–Robert Owens, Saint-Simon, Bronson Alcott, the Oneida colony, the Quakers, who trace their philosophy back to Christ. The point is to convince by example rather than by bayonet, molotov cocktail, or linked charges of

TNT. To form a community whose values are so sterling, results so eye-popping, that the rest of the population will come over and do likewise. Thoreau, a latecomer to the field, had the same notion, but several graduate students have informed me he was lousy in the sack. Jesus Christ, the grand-daddy of the Utopian proselytizers, was such a schlemiel about revolutionary survival tactics, we know what happened to him. It took Peter to Bolshevize that Utopian revolution and turn it into a thriving open shop.'

Frederick Engels, at Marx's behest, overturned all that with *Socialism, Utopian and Scientific* and thus was bred the notion of revolutionary humanism–a contradiction in terms, and we know where that has led. The Utopian tomato commune was founded to return us all to the idea of socialism by example, each one teach one, share out the chores and divvy up the goods, democratic grassroots parliament, rump court, town meeting vote and collectivity all down the line. Besides, there is nothing like the savor of a ripe Jersey tomato when you're fresh up from the beach in August. We hoped, by example, to bring over the whole world.

Our founding manifesto, engraved in 36 point Bodoni bold on the cornerstone of the all-important latrine and sewage treatment plant, chiseled by a well-spoken North Carolina cemetery stonecutter, read in part:

> "The French revolution, Paris Commune, Russian, Cuban, let us not mention Nicaraguan revolutions led us only to a world of greedy, mean inhumanity, an eastern Europe gutted of its art. The failure of the planned economy to deliver the goods and enlighten the species has brought about a failure of belief in the fundamental humanistic prayer. We are founded therefore on the premise of blind unaccountable faith in the latent intrinsic good of the entire species–its capacity to learn by doing, to

> share and share alike and show and tell. We believe in the vitality, though it may be far-fetched, of democratically exercised free will. You, too, comrade, can learn to understand the higher beauty of a slurp on a ripe tomato, walking hand in hand with your honey on the beach on a moonlit night. May all our atomic suns be defused, swords into plowshares, blather, blather, mucky-muck, amen."

To estimate the extent of Utopian lands, some of us traversed the fields at night. Forty acres in tomatoes, I say, Maxine says seventy, Psi eighty-five, Epsilon fifty, Rho stays out of it. We all argue. It must be more than that. That's just the tomato fields. There's also the pasture–grazing land–ten acres? Twenty? Epsilon is a slob at figures. I myself understand very little that comes before differential calculus and the derivation of the fraction form of "pi." Somebody in the central committee has all the right figures. We could settle our disputes in an instant, but we'd for the most part rather not. One half acre or is it two of corn, green beans, squash and eggplant for the use of the collective, unless eggplant was dropped this season–probably not, a lot are vegetarians, as that's been written up in "Radical Chic". It might be green beans that were dropped. We might raise elephants, damn it, if not this year than maybe next. Perhaps we already have or pterodactyls, god help us, if they'll help support the cause. But no, cows, it seems–a modicum of DDT-free milk. Chickens in roomy little huts. It's all been done for years. Saint-Simon, for Christ's sake, planted eggs in bushes and he watched the birdies fly. Fourier kicked his mother in the soft underbelly to prove that man could really do it–it was just the money system held us back. Like Upton Sinclair's EPIC, they got by on scrip. Certain Quaker communes a thousand years ago were known to harbor little boats that plied the Seine and tried to win over converts to a closed-mouth passive resistance policy against "auto da fe". So the possibilities are always there, or was it all made up?

For a time I was seeing Rho. His room was larger than most at that end of the quad. He had a great many books on genetic intervention and the plan of DNA. He did not talk about this to me or to anyone else. He planted his tomatoes as did we all. There was a certain position, on a Shaker hard-back chair, with my feet locked into the spokes in the back. We tolerated this no more than once every two weeks.

The fields went well enough. There had been much talk about compost, animal manure, human contributions, treated and so forth. All that had to be discussed at the outset. Then there was no more to say.

To fulfill the funding agency's requirements, natural insecticides had to be found. The government, we learned, was fond of financing groups that meant to overthrow it, to study them, find out how it's done. We guessed they were grateful that we only meant to set a good example, to overthrow, as it were, by teams of fours and violets. We were rolling in grants. There was a certain amount of interest in discovering ways to disrupt the mating procedures of the more virulent aphids. We trained the aphid cows in the tricks of liberated ball-busting. The pricks of the little green males withered on the vine. Both sides agreed to give up bearing young. For several years at a clip this had a beneficial effect on the crops. We filed a report with the agency and exaggerated our results.

The last time I avoided a steering-committee meeting I went for a walk with Maxine. Sometimes on these walks she performed certain services which Rho preferred not to do. Once there was something about her breast nudging my armpit that Rho and the others could only simulate. Maxine began about the sunset.

"The deep purple of the streaks of clouds against the fiery red ball," she said.

"I think the streaks are black," I said.

"No. The sky is blue, the sun, at this point, blood red, hence purple, with mauve at the wispy edges."

"I don't like to be testy," I said. "But it's the silhouette effect. What you see is the shadowed side of the clouds. The sun is partially eclipsed. But I might grant purple–mauve, if you must–at the edges."

"All right then. But as for streaks. Don't you think that's so inadequate?"

"What would you have?"

"Mares' tails usually indicate the wispy parts."

"That implies a horse's asshole also on the scene. Did you mean the sun?"

"Like streamers in the wind."

"Rags at a witch's skirt?"
"The devil's pennants."
"Flags for the new order, it seems."
"Similes are so inadequate."
"Aren't we all."

Sometimes I discuss these matters with Psi. Often he prefers to stand on his head. He mutters something about yoga and the flow of blood to the brain.

I ask him what we'll do if the collective breaks up.

"Other things."

"It'll be much the same?"

"Much the same," he said. "I'll do headstands at street corners to help with other people's meetings."

We all applauded Psi's headstands except those too weak, too old, too young, too bored to applaud. Sometimes I would have thought to count myself in one of those categories. If it had been anyone else. But Psi. I applauded always faithfully, a small bit, not too ostentatious, stopping work in the fields, leaving off the tending of basil, the tasting or non-tasting of tomatoes. He would bunch himself up into a ball, from which he slowly uncurled to extend legs as thin as the night air in Denver. Wrapped in bindings of softest cotton velour, machine washable, ribboned in colors of mauve, heliotrope, aquamarine. These seemingly changing in the sun. For the sun would sometimes halt directly above a wavering kneecap on its way across the pellucid blue of sky. Once up in the air there was never a waver. A steady upthrust like a tower of light, like a cone of destiny, like a steeple of the temple of higher occult knowledge. A deeply religious experience for all those susceptible to that sort of thing. So I'm told by visitors. All of us are way past that stage and beyond all hope. Sometimes Psi branched off into handstands, lifting himself ever so carefully up on two hands, the barest chance he might miss, we all watched with breath bated. At the very end when he balanced atop one hand as delicately as a cattail in a willow pond, as gracefully as two dragonflies mating in midair, he would raise a little sign: UTOPIA. That was the end of his show. Then back down on two hands, head and two hands for resting, then back up again. The small sign waving: UTOPIA, only that. We wound up with many recruits, but we didn't know what to do with them, so we sent them to Epsilon to hear lectures on the morphology of certain "tropistic diseases."

Epsilon was having a hard time enjoying the vine-ripened tomatoes. We had them every year. Bushels. I had long since given it up. My taste buds had at the outset been as alert as anyone's. Years pass. I could still notice a radish now and then, but the tomatoes, no, they required an onion. In truth it was not entirely the tomatoes, not entirely the aging, not entirely growing stale from years of the Utopian community and fresh ripe tomatoes. The manure committee had met to explain to us all why this year's tomatoes were better nourished than commercial varieties. Since the human waste recycling project we had all been exhorted to eat more wheat germ and dairy products–calcium–for the good of the tomatoes. Attendance at that meeting had been mandatory. I tried playing gin rummy mentally. It was always the same meeting, but never before such a push on tomatoes. As part of an ideological campaign we were each to take a stint explaining on cable TV why our Utopian tomatoes were superior. I tried to say I couldn't taste them. It wasn't the fault of the tomatoes, I was sure, but the aging taste buds. Now I'm even having a hard time when there's onion.

Psi solved the problem by doing headstands for his part in a Utopian tomato distribution at factory gates. Some use-value was ascribed to this which he reluctantly acquiesced in, namely that the Utopian life could lead to a healthier physique, some such, I'm sure, Psi neglected to give me details, i.e., the tomatoes could enhance headstanding performance. Psi persisted in waggling his feet to get laughs, to some good effect. Epsilon has joined me in surreptitiously going off milk and wheat germ. We never discuss the possible results on the manure.

Epsilon went about hopelessly pining for his first wife, Melinda Sweetwater; I pined for Epsilon; Rho for me, Maxine for Rho, and so on, Psi mostly staying out of it. We were thus all thoroughly indulging the despair of unrequited love, happy in our grief as otters in kelp, Psi headstanding, Epsilon remorselessly droning on and on, Maxine and Rho and I nudging and lolly-gagging, when, over the dunes, charged a delegation from the Utopian Collective Central Committee, led by the magnificent elected official, raven-silk hair blowing back, the truly remarkable Du Wop, leader of us all.

"We charge Epsilon with male chauvinism in the first degree," Du Wop intoned severely as she and the collective leadership approached. "We are here to conduct a fair and orderly trial."

To control my outrage and endear myself to the heart of my recalcitrant beloved, I offered to stand as defense counsel to the baffled Epsilon. "What is the basis for this charge at this time?" I asked discreetly, not wanting to put myself too far out on a limb, even granted the efficacies of representative democracy.

"Melinda Sweetwater has absconded with top-secret collective information," Du Wop charged. "What we eat all day so the manure collective can grow a richer crop. If Epsilon were a true communard, he would have won her over to the cause. If he had understood the ideals he could have communicated the ideals. What, pray forbid, would have become of any children he might have had by this fat-ass broad, Melinda Sweetwater?"

"Here, here," I said and I addressed my remarks not only to Du Wop but to the entire commission. "It is a well known fact that Epsilon has lectured duly on the ideals of the commune, the poignancy of tomatoes laced with basil, the efficacy of wheat germ and calcium in the shit, every day since the commune began, three times a day regularly as Ex-Lax, when the quarter hour strikes. Although Melinda Sweetwater did not attend these lectures, it is known that she did type up his notes."

"It is also known," Du Wop further charged, "that Epsilon habitually picks out one chick from each lecture series to wink at, and in the privacy of the conference room, encourages her to bleat out oaths of undying love." Du Wop, proud of herself on this one, pounded her gavel to the rhythm of the surrounding sea.

"Is this true?" I whispered, distraught, to Epsilon, though I would not divulge to him the cause of my alarm. I can countenance infidelity, open marriage, the search for perfect partners, but I would not for the world be caught dead falling in love with a man every third woman in the commune already had her heart set on. It is a point of pride with me that I generally fall for men who are difficult to love.

"Well," said Epsilon. He hung his head, I thought, a bit sheepishly. "It's hard to keep up the good word, the lectures day in day out new world coming and on like that when they yawn and snap their gum. Just the first one who responds...."

"Womanizer," thundered Du Wop. "Breaker of hearts. Families have been divided. Suicide attempts. Country houses lost. Children driven mad with the pain of Mama's ache.

"We are each responsible for our own actions," I said, taking up, now, Epsilon's brief. "Nobody asked them sir," she said.

"Let me tell you what it feels like," said Du Wop. "Do you want to know what it feels like?"

There was a look of pain on Du Wop's face. I saw her weaken. I knew when to keep my mouth shut in Epsilon's behalf.

"When I was a child," said Du Wop, "in junior high, I was very smart. Everybody I knew said the same line to me. Smart girls scare me. Shave your legs, why don't you, and get yourself some armpit goo. Don't talk so many syllables and maybe I'll take you to the Roxy for some popcorn and we'll sit in the balcony where I can cop a feel. I have come to the conclusion–it is no longer even the pain of my existence–that you cannot read disquisitions on Roland Barthes and get a good blow job on the same rainy indoor day. If life is this unfair to women, why should this dude get off scot free?"

"Melinda never liked her," I whispered to Epsilon out of earshot of the great Du Wop.

"How's that?" he said. Was I hinting that I knew more about his wife than he did and did that make him boil?

"We worked together," I reminded him. "On the cabbage line in Pismo. She used to say the damnedest things."

I was torn. It would not serve me well with regard to my teeming love for Epsilon to have him stew in ex-wife juice into eternity. On the other hand, sometimes catharsis is the better way, taking the bull by the tail, as it were, looking the facts in the face. Of prime consideration was Epsilon's security. Mine was nothing if not an unselfish love–a healing love, I intended; a safe harbor, I would bill myself, a port in a storm. Above all, we must not remind the great Du Wop about Melinda Sweetwater and her stealing the plans to the human manure project. Epsilon would surely be implicated.

Fortunately, Du Wop was lost in her own reveries. "You try to talk to them," she said, "read to them aloud passages from Thomas Mann. Hell, I like a good lay as well as any goony tart, but jeez, they don't let the words get out you mouf. They stuff it full of cock."

"All palaver and what they can get from you," I said, to make, tentatively, the bond.

"What's in it for you?" said Du Wop, suddenly stern, as if she, not I, had become, with this trial, the disposer of Epsilon's ungodly soul.

"I want to bear Epsilon's child, but sshh, don't tell him yet. I want it to be a surprise."

Du Wop thought a bit, stroked a beard she would have had had she been born a man, said at last, "The commune needs more kids. Productivity is low. I'll strike a deal. The kid in return for clemency. You raise your kid on the commune to share and share alike and we drop the Melinda Sweetwater secret-stealing charge."

"You're on, babe," I said and we winked at each other knowingly and slapped each other five.

Epsilon was so happy that he kissed me and I lingered at his touch, my crotch set all aquiver at the barest brush of lip at cheek.

2

The Professional Revolutionist came to talk to me about leaving my Utopian ways and bringing my group over to the full-time fight for the revolution. What do you think of the basil, I said. He lit a Havana cigar with a twist of paper from the kitchen stove. One of the comrades adds basil to his stash, he said. He offered me a position at the upper echelons with say in the national policy. Together we went out to secure a series of blue stakes to hold up the bobbing dahlias. He promised me all the Havana cigars I could choke on.

One of the workers from the nearby canning factory was interested in becoming a Professional

Revolutionist

"The Professional Revolutionist wears a bit of red somewhere about his person at all times," he was told. "This red grows wild in some gardens, is cultivated in others."

"I have very little red in my garden, but we have, of course, the tomatoes."

"We don't have Bingo," said the Professional Revolutionist, "but ham and swiss, hold the mayo."

In the war against the bureaucratic type, the Professional Revolutionist was good at jogging and jump-rope and taught me the tricks of reading hot type upside down and backwards, how to correct proofs.

"At the beginning of the last revolution," he said, "there were fiercely loyal little bands who leapt across the mountainside playing on their windbags a multiracial tune. We still consider the viability of that revolution, although they're waiting for a larger country to come along."

"But there is always all that watching the sun rise and set, rise and set, as it does again and again," Maxine said, "and the stars come out at night, or else it's cloudy and you don't see them, but always the dark, the phases of the moon, scraps and shreds of clouds moving across the face. You get up to see it and you hold hands or you don't or you stay in bed thumping about or sleeping it off getting ready for another time, but it's still the same, the never-ending up and down of it."

"Precisely why," the Professional Revolutionist said, "that is indeed why I make this offer."

"Well" I said, "I have to admit–all that breathing in and breathing out."

"One foot up," said Epsilon, with a chortley wistful sigh.

"The other foot down," said Rho, pale pinko cock limp now in his hand.

"AND THAT IS THE WAY TO LONDON TOWN." we all said in chorus, Psi waggling, handstanding, bare toes as rosy as the rosy-toed dawn into the red morning sky.

"Half a life," said the Professional Revolutionist, "is not worth living."

"I beg to disagree," I said. "I don't think you'll win us with your ways. I beg to disagree."

"Beg a little harder," said the Professional Revolutionist. "Put in all your heart and soul. I want to hear you beg. I would even like you down on your knees. Nothing serious, politically, is meant by that, you understand. It's just what turns me on. Makes the cock to crow. Just consider–when I was a lowly child, even when I won at dodge ball, recess time, nobody paid me no nevermind. Now that I am a Professional Revolutionist, organizing my life to be in the forefront of the struggle–but safely protected from direct bayonet attack by the warm bodies of the rank and file–when the prick rises an entire universe salutes–that is in the scheme. As I said, the alternative is half-life, like radiation, every day you experience half your allotment trickle out between your toes."

"Oh?" said Maxine, and I thumped her on the back encouragingly. "True leadership, like good parenting, demands the building up and pushing forth of budlings even in your stead."

"I overheard," Maxine went on, "a garden slug from a tomato plant talking to a dung beetle from Basil 3, saying, 'Hell, I'll take any kind of life, just let me push this slime as long as I'm allowed.'"

"I've made a certain investment," said the Professional Revolutionist. "What if I have the power to save the race from doom? What if all I can ever do is add my little bit to it? What if I live a full life and get laid a lot along the way? As it happens, I sired a daughter, last heard passed around from hand to hand wrapped up in a paper doily and placed at a variety of doorsteps nestled in a breadbasket from the time she was three months old. Wound up in a parcel post station, picked up by the granddaughter of a fat Malaysian princess, and raised in a day camp for commie brats up in Croton, New York, next door to Eugene O'Neill."

"I agree with Maxine," I said. "No hard feelings. I thank you for your sperm, your hard cock spurting inside Mommy's tummy. I would much prefer to be born at all than to live life as a rock. Though there are times, there are times. 'Make me a mandrake,' an overpotent guy I once knew said, 'Some insensate object in this place.' 'I like the life,' I said, 'the breathing in and breathing out, the pull of cool air in the lungs when you've swum several laps in the commune pool alongside your second son.' For that, I guess I have your ilk to thank. For the rest, I'm glad I owe you not a drop of blood or sweat or tears or even rage, have nothing more to thank, or curse, or piss on. We start fresh, just who we are. I guess I'm grateful now for that. As to the rest. Fuck off.'"

"Wait," said the Professional Revolutionist. "Wait up a half a mo'. I saved my best line for the last. The explanation for my whole existence."

"Hear, hear," said Epsilon. "This better be a good one. My father preferred the company of whores and hashslingers, recruited them to the cause, left me and Mama home at night to play strip poker by the hour. Then run off when I was ten to hoist the red flag and sing Solidarity Forever as if that way he could force back the unremitting gloom."

"Epsilon," I said, as an aside, "You're an orphan of the revolution, too? There are a few of us. We all surreptitiously celebrate Christmas at my digs every year–Jews and orphan Reds, parlor pinks alike. I'd so gladly–you can't imagine how gladly–have you officiate at the carving of the joint."

"Too painful to contemplate," said Epsilon and turned his face away. After a moment, he looked back.

"Try to understand," Epsilon moaned. "The revolution defathered me. The unfathering unmanned me. Melinda Sweetwater left me because I couldn't add our checkbook up and would never know how to repair an electric lamp."

"Epsilon, I appeal to you, like existential babies, we can start fresh and father and mother each other in the right way. I have long since mastered the calculus of checkbooks and can teach you–I'm a gentle teacher, Epsilon, I swear I am. I'd leave your dignity intact. I've had to be both father and mother to myself since I was three months old–with some help along the way. The first thing I did when I had a summer place with Schreier was rewire all the lamps. Oh, Epsilon, come away with me. We'll both chip in. Fuck the revolution. Fuck the commune, even. Fuck Du Wop, Rho, Maxine, and Psi. We get our own little shack by a trout stream in the woods and spend our nights beside an open fire unraveling the mysteries of the polarity of three-way switches."

"How many psychiatrists," said Maxine shyly, "does it take to change a light bulb? Give up?" Rho nodded in the direction of Maxine's creamy neck, not caring what she said. "Only one," she said, "but it takes a very long time because the light bulb has to want to change."

"You're missing the point," said the Professional Revolutionist. "I have bumper stickers, two-dollar buttons, two different slogans, take your pick:

THE MASS OF MEN LEAD
LIVES OF QUIET DESPERATION.

THE UNEXAMINED LIFE IS NOT WORTH LIVING"

"The revolutionary life is the answer to all that, said the Professional Revolutionist. Step right up now, my leaflets will explain."

"Surely you must see by now, oh, dearest dear," I whispered fondly, nudging up to Epsilon. "The life your father fled is the selfsame life you in your turn are fleeing, too, in your fashion, the life of pushing all that slime. Is that what you see in the life I offer you?"

Angrily, without reply, Epsilon thrust me most meanly to one side.

Had I tried to know him too easily? Come on, in my great need, too strong? I approached him once again.

"Black birch in the fire at night, I said, gives a tang of mint to the moonlit air. I can teach you how to recognize the bark." I tried to take his hand in mine. Resistant, he pulled away. "You are lured by the Professional Revolutionist's campaign," I said.

"Not a bit of it," he said. "You scare me." He went on, "Mama, my sole comfort and support, always told me people get electrocuted trying to rewire their own lamps."

"It is true," I said, chagrined, "I have had a few

bad experiences rewiring my own lamps. Damn near charred myself to death on more than one occasion. Then I learned the trick. You pull the plug out, first, darling, and then it's all all right. I'm near to setting up a school. Have several candidates in mind. Wanted to give you first crack, I always loved you so. But life is possible, sometimes sweet enough, without love. Don't worry–I'll go on. I won't make the same mistakes again. Maybe others."

3

In a spirit of mutual cooperation, the farm-factory collective decided to work together on a picnic.

Detail assigned to bring:

Potato salad.

Deviled eggs.

Assorted cold cuts.

Beer and soda.

Detail assigned to bring Negro sympathizers.

What's a picnic without a softball game?

Side bets on the running-dog lackey races.

At night, a campfire, with marshmallows and Peat Bog Soldiers.

Doesn't this make the work more fun. Doesn't

this make the work more fun.

The picnic was decided on collectively. Epsilon was the first of our group to dissent.

"We must keep it just ourselves," he said, "just the ones were in it first."

Du Wop, mindful of the grand design, was the champion in favor of bringing over the canning factory. "There's a show of interest from the leader of the worker's collective," she said. "Rather a cute little shlong, if you ask me, but he won't listen to a thing I say. Shows no respect. I thought perhaps we'd brain him on the public field–in softball, say, and show our team's still champs."

"The picnic," Epsilon said. He stammered, looked at me. A warmth shot up my groin as I gave the high five, urged him on. He had never looked to Melinda Sweetwater for reassurance about his ideological stance, I knew–just how to file his notes. Perhaps I was growing on him after all.

"The picnic," he said, "must be a time of reunification, healing up, mending fences." (With a softball bat? I wondered). "We must show how well we work together."

"Epsilon," Du Wop scolded, "we have a real opportunity here to prove the efficacy of the theory of subversion by example. We want to show it is theoretically possible to win over the workers collective just by the glow of the love in our hearts and the gleam of our ripe tomatoes, with basil added for the taste."

I spoke up, with bile, once again in Epsilon's behalf. "We're weary of the recruitment campaign," I said. "The ever-present need to win them over, make them act a certain way–aren't they, just as we, bailed out on their own recognizance? Let them act any way they choose."

"Our lives may be at stake in the long run," Du Wop said tersely.

I'm afraid I lost my temper and grew rather mean.

"You just want to go all shock-em-up competitive because your one Cute Shlong couldn't get a mental hard-on and listen to what you had to say.

"Fuck it, Du Wop," I said, "you're just a sore-ass twat like all the rest. I want no part."

Du Wop, at this, I'm afraid, was in such a rage she was spitting all the bullets she could bite.

Maxine, to ameliorate, stepped forth while Rho and Psi from opposite angles patted down the flustered feathers of my rump.

"Why don't we try a square dance?" Maxine offered. "Good old-fashioned ho-down. Four-in-hand, Hora, Bunny-Hop, Group Grope and the mincing do-si-do."

"I don't dance a step," said Epsilon sadly. "Never did. Melinda always had to dance with other dudes. I always prayed she imagined it was me, though I don't really think she did."

"It's simple," I said. "Just like fucking, only standing up. I know you know how to do that."

"All those people watching," Epsilon moaned. He was close to tears.

"Du Wop," I challenged. "You never taught this poor bloke how to dance, all the years he was over on your side? Nor wire his own lamp? Nor drive a car?" (I had it on good authority he still could not do that.) "Shit, cunt, what you been doin with these boys? No wonder they gets left."

"Don't, don't" Epsilon pleaded. "Don't get her mad at you. I don't want to get caught between the two of you."

"Why not, love," I murmured softly in return. "Looks like she's got fine legs, and as for me, why, just as soon as I can lose a little weight...."

"The committee has decided then," Du Wop cut in.

I hadn't heard a vote either hands up or roll call as the by-laws called for but Du Wop was already as pissed at me as I wanted her to get.

"Softball is definitely in–by executive order," Du Wop said. "To be played competitively against Cute Shlong's cannery collective team. To be followed by potluck supper, dishes collectively from our side–to be determined, who cooks what, by decision of the central committee–individualistically from the cannery collective. We all eat together and share alike then dance our stupid heads off into the night. It's all been decided on. Don't even think about voting."

"Maxine," she said, stepping away from our group, "any time you'd like a spot on the central committee...I'm in a position to curry certain favors...we could use a shrewd mediator."

Maxine blushed and turned her back.

All right then, the strategy was decided, the war plan mapped. We would win over the first factory collective by a combination of superior softball, macaroni in tomato-basil sauce, and group grope on the dance floor to a live collective band. Who knows, with any luck, if we live long enough, if the planet holds and ozone permits, we could whomp up a huge vat of tomato-basil sauce and do-si-do the world.

It turned out that the canning factory was eager to join forces with the Utopian community. The factory committee, which had just replaced the employers, the old owners, and seventeen boards of directors, was representative of all major ethnic groupings in proportion to the factory population–mostly black and Puerto Rican women. We had an equal number of groupings on our side as well, although neither Epsilon, Psi, Rho, Maxine, nor I had been asked at the outset to participate in planning sessions, and we all took note of that.

"We got your tomatoes at the plant gates."

"There was that one who stands on his head."

"A professional revolutionist came by and read aloud from Andre Gorz."

"We thought we should have a say in the product of our labor."

"If not now, then when?"

"The days aren't getting any slower."

"You produce a damned decent tomato, is what we mean to say, and, well, if you'll have a spot to spare, we'd like to join in, do you know what we mean?"

"When I was very little in Puerto Rico, I would

run through the mud in the sugar cane fields when the rain came down, drops the size of quarters, and I often would suck on the sweet tomato but not so good as the way you do it here with the compost and other materials we hear about."

"Back home in North Carolina a boy was lynched for mixing certain vegetables on an ancestral gravestone on the wrong side of the cemetery. Somebody smash splattery tomato soup on the memory of my grandmother's diadem, but we formed a movement to put a stop to that."

"For my part, I prefer pumpkins. I'm only along for the ride. Perhaps at a later time."

"We thought if only we could help a bit to spread the news."

I was deeply moved and offered fresh basil, an indispensable ingredient to the potentially canned (or jarred) tomatoes under negotiation.

"Nonetheless," I said, "we have certain trepidations. I'm not so new to this. My mother, unlike other girls her age, climbed up a grapevine wrapped around a California shrub oak from which vantage point along with a suck on sweet apricots, she foresaw the collectivization of the entire garment industry, and the gray faces of women at work down through the ages. Certain of us were asked to alter the pattern of our favorite dance step in keeping with the times."

"The ten-twelve, diez-doce, sugar cane is jefe de la crop."

"It could stand a bit of radish."

"Apples and bananas were never passed around in the school I went to on the wrong side of the tracks."

"John Steinbeck told us once," said the leader, Du Wop's Cute Shlong, "that Russian wolfhounds refused to wag their tails when questioned by certain committees, but Big Sur wasn't born when some heads were rolling overseas. It was harder, in those days, just to scratch for bread, but those times could come around again."

"My father before he died, asked me never to have his child. We were eighteen in a bed at the time. It was hard to tell which was which."

"My daddy was a bayou boat man who never thought he'd grow so tired of the stench of cabbage mass produced and brought too soon to market. Not that he minded much but he killed a nest of water moccasins attacking a certain woman's dog and what thanks did he get when he needed it? There never has been the chance before, and Frederick Engels told me in a dream that I should, so I would like to take the chance to join."

"I'm growing itchy at this news," I said, "if it wasn't for Epsilon and certain others. But I do like the taste of basil with the canned tomatoes, and Maxine, by rubbing with a special knob at the discs between the vertebrae convinced me to further share the joy."

The cannery collective softball team, just for fun, called themselves the *Niggerspics*, came equipped with team jackets 1950s style, red and black with the word *Niggerspics* emblazoned on the backs, in gold script, on a field of royal red.

Cute Shlong, the leader of the *Niggerspics*, was a blond, freckle-faced overgrown boy, a genetic throwback, with a fishing rod slung over his shoulder in a special holster that left him free to pitch.

Psi, our first baseman, could bat as well as catch just with his feet.

Rho was our catcher, hunkering down, his poor sore prick webbed in its own silken niche.

Du Wop coached our side firmly with a quiet

antisentimental style that yet always, always, commandeered respect.

The umpire, the most oppressed of both groups, therefore the ultimate authority, was a thirteen-year-old village girl, retarded, a Native American black pregnant prostitute, gay, of course, and addicted to crack.

As the Professional Revolutionist was our only media connection, we gave him the mike. THE *NIGGERSPICS,* he blasted out, HAVE SURMOUNTED THEIR EXPLOITATION AND ARE IN PRIME POSITION FOR CATCHING HIGH FLY POPS.

Epsilon and I, due to our retrograde positions on male chauvinism and the need for right-line recruitment drives and our general defiance of Du Wop's tireless authority, were last in the batting lineup. For his part, Cute Shlong pitched ball, like woo, with a slow and vital verve that Du Wop creamed at. Cute Shlong, Du Wop had told us, had the teensiest organ in captivity. He made up for this with political savvy, an almost correct line on the woman question, and, on the softball field, a virile athletic grace. He took his time, nice and slow and easy, walkin' like he walkin' on sof' boil' eggs.

For Epsilon and me, in sweatsuits and sneakers

at the last bench in the dugout, this meant time for talk.

For my part, I had intended to take the pressure off, lay off the mush. I launched just for the relief, into my usual riff for such occasions.

"Don't be surprised if I strike out every time," I said. "It's important to know what that early orphanage has done to us, but god help us, not to dwell, the point is to get free–well, I never learned all this shit when I was young. Was the same true of you? I was a dud kid, couldn't roller skate, would lose my mark at hopscotch, always tripped in jump-rope. Couldn't even ride a bike or drive a car 'til I was thirty. Schreier had to teach me. That and chess. The first sport I was even passably good at was sex. Was that true of you?"

There. A smile. But Epsilon scratched his head.

"There's something I've been wanting to ask you," he said. "We seem to have some time, what with Psi up there standing on his hands. It'll take Cute Shlong quite a while, I warrant, to figure out the strike zone on him and get that umpire girl to call."

"Shoot," I said. "I'm your girl. Do with me what you will."

"Hold on, he said. "Hold up. Slow down. I

didn't mean to commit myself to that."

"What then?" I said.

"All I wanted was to know what your program was, your platform that you're running on–your life plan, as it were, for me."

"Mutuality." I said. "That easy, shared affection, holding hands while we read each other's computer printouts. Maybe, if we're lucky, love."

"Why me?" he said. "Why do you glom all over me? What made you pick me out?"

"I'm not sure why myself. I know it all adds up. I feel it in my bones. I ache. I weep. I laugh. I know whatever else I do you will always be the man I have it for. I won't be fair to any other man. But if you turn me down, there *will* be others and I'll just be unfair. The act can be, if you make it, ninety percent of the fact. I will always know you will always be the one to the nth power for me. I seem somehow to be branded on the backside with the name of Epsilon's Girl."

"That's pretty heavy, babe. I don't know if I can handle that."

"Not too heavy," I said. "Two men have said the same sort of thing to me; I to one other before you, dead lo, three, four years. You didn't think either one of us was kids."

Epsilon scratched his head again, seemed to find words hard to say.

"Babies?" he croaked out.

"Babies. Okay. Babies. I'm an old bitch in a dry season. My dugs, sucked out by Alex Schreier's spawn, are no longer perky creamy orbs. I've had my little tadpoles, as they say. The two. I don't need more for me. Those guys are grown to frat-boys, sharking up coeds' skirts in Harvard Square. Not necessarily following the right line. Frog E. and Toad. More, I don't need for me, but you have the distinct aroma of a man who needs a father-needing child so you can come to manhood. I've known men that way. Mostly abandoned boys stretched tall. You can smell the fathering need on them the way you can smell wild onion in the dung of cows. However, as they say, my tubes are tied. I may have eggs but I'm afraid they're stale. We'd have to seek out some novel way–in vitro. My womb's still sound, we could later ask a surrogate to babysit. Pick up a matched set across the Colombian border cheaper than cocaine. Melinda Sweetwater wanted a full-grown man to ride her. She complained often enough to me. I could tell it in her voice. She would confide in me *ad infinitum* while trimming cabbage leaves and singing raucous songs. I want a full-growed man by my side, too, but I'm willing to train him up. Other people's mother's jobs have left me sick at heart."

"But how," said Epsilon. "Details. Facts. Where would I stow my socks. File cabinets, lecture notes, books, I need to know. Typewriter, carbon paper, paper clips, and so on. I'd like a private phone. I may want to call up an old girl."

"As it happens," I said, "thanks to the untold rather bizarre sexual favors I performed for Alex Schreier at odd hours of the day and night for nearly eighteen years, for which, you better believe, I made him pay me smartly, I am heir to a four-bedroom apartment at cheap rent in a pleasant tree-lined section of the commune where there are good babysitters, good schools, good playgrounds, built-in laundry, adequate shopping, and excellent reception on cable TV.

My set are what the Cubans call '*responsables*'–teachers, social workers, film editors, Herman Melville fans, some down from the Red Bronx, a little writing or painting on the side. And then my private nest of buddies, kooks and waifs, single folk, for whom I fry up chicken parts twice each summer. They bring wine and cheese and fruit and we camp out in the July and August heat for Shakespeare-in-the-Park–the only amusement, aside from hugs and foul-mouthed jokes, we can all, even chipping in, afford. This takes our attention away from the fact that anti-depressants drastically impair sexual functioning and increase weight, and all of us have lost, irrevocably, it seems, the main loves of our lives. I wouldn't mind more dough than I have now, even if it means longer stints at the International Harvester, plowing Basil 3. Babies eat up funds. We must be realistic. Schreier had the stuff in spades but doled it out at whim. I remember once Frog E. had a birthday coming up. I had no toy and candy loot. Would I want him to one day complain to shrinks of this? Schreier said I spoiled the brat what did he need it for just squandering his father's hatefully earned bread I was only making up for my own childhood abscesses. And that might very well have been that. Pulling back the blankets, raging close to tears that I had no income of my own to lavish on my birthday tad, I saw Schreier's naked cock in blossom. I gave it to him good, bobbing down on him, so sweet, like any geisha girl, sucking nice and kind, bile and venom filling up the molars I had to hold apart. At breakfast, he forked over fifty bucks. I caught on fast. Other times, made more; still others, not so much. That was just what I had to do–would have to do again–for anybody's brat I bore. Now that Schreier's gone I'm piss poor broke as hell. My integrity, I suppose is what keeps the empty bed half-warm–but leaves my cunt forlorn. If you think you do want kids, well, hell, I don't care if you're unfaithful, but you don't take away my spawn. If we're in this, and you mean it, and there are kids involved, at our age, it's for the duration or else just don't sign on. We can always scratch each other's ass as friends–or not. It's up to you. For my part, I would indeed want a life–Europe-vaunting and such muck, but warming up what's left with maybe a Chevy van big enough for kids and pals and country shit. You'd have to learn to drive, and cook outdoors and mix an extremely dry gimlet with a twist–that's how these things are done. Du Wop and Psi and the rest as uncles and aunties–your Melinda Sweetwater, too, if she's a mind...well, hell...I think you're up at bat."

"I'll think about it," Epsilon said. "Leave a memo with my secretary in the morning." Then, enigmatically, with a secret smile, he chucked me with his forefinger underneath my chin. "Youse is a good kid, Dinny Dimwit," he said as he adjusted his batting helmet, and I purred all through my flesh.

Not long afterward, I heard over the loudspeaker the boom of the Professional Revolutionist's best rabble-rousing voice: GROUND-RULES DOUBLE FOR THE UTOPIAN SIDE. TWO RUNNERS BATTED IN. BATTER SAFE AT SECOND. LOOKS LIKE OLD EPSILON'S OUR NEXT WORKER'S HERO.

Du Wop kissed him, as I saw, when the game was won by Epsilon's two points. Psi, Rho, and Maxine each slapped him five. Even Cute Shlong came over and patted Epsilon's behind, which gratified Du Wop–she had got her vengeance back.

I, for my part, slunk off by myself to check the tomato-basil vats.

4

After the dinner, the macaroni in tomato-basil sauce from our side, as mentioned; potato salad, fried chicken and diced multiculturalists in a sauce from theirs–no hard liquor, apple jack and cranberry juice mixed with ginger-ale, huge chunks of iced martini with picks, Epsilon was called upon to give a speech. Even at that, we knew the speech was a cover, a sop, to keep us busy while Du Wop and Cute Shlong met with the cannery collective and delegates from the *Niggerspics* to settle the vegetarian question behind our backs.

We knew even as we sat there that they, on the pretext of representing our best interests, would determine the question of whether all the rest of us should stop eating meat, stop raising meat, eradicating meat from human gluttons' wet dreams. Some punk party brat among us had started all this off–we had all just gone along till now–a girl of four or five asking that perennial question they all ask: "If they're so cute and cuddly and furry and barnyard forest friends the way they have them in those books, why do we eat them for dinner and perform our experiments on them?"

This is not so hard to answer as it seems. I whispered to Epsilon and Maxine one night while I drove them to Bare Ass mountain in the commune's Chevy van so they could make out in the back seat. If Epsilon could drive the van himself, it would save a lot of grief.

"All you have to do," I said, "is, as I told the head editor in the children's book collective where I sometimes do odd jobs, is put out a new kiddie book, *Ma, We Having Floyd For Dinner Again, Tonight?"* But nobody ever listens to me, they just like a good laugh and to be a bit aroused, so we wound up with this mess on our hands.

Epsilon was enjoined by Du Wop not to mention the vegetarian question. Du Wop was in league, again this week, with Cute Shlong. It was to be settled by the combined collective leadership of the new vanguard, and democratic centralism, you better believe it, would be strictly enforced.

Bored, restless, all knowing that in private, our mealtime fate was being decided for us, we tried to listen to Epsilon drone on. Maxine bobbed dutifully along the ridges of Rho's ever-erect cock so he wouldn't snore. Psi held a collection basket perennially aloft from his headstanding perch. I took notes and prepared some smart-sounding questions to ask to bolster Epsilon, let him think we cared what he had to say.

Epsilon's subject matter was the DNA molecule, conscious control of the autonomic nervous system, and the prospects for immortality. Although this seemed a likely subject, several young cannery workers in the back row took out nail files, and, snapping gum, diligently set to work. Nobody exactly threw spitballs, but mash notes were passed around the room. There were smirks and smothered jeers. Several of the smarter of our own collective were doing their homework for their next class where the teacher was stricter. I saw my chance–I gazed up fondly, with a look of respectful challenge and intelligent wonder on my face. While I have not been a dewy-cheeked young lovely in lo many years, this look–bottled now by Estee Lauder, is available at the campus store. Poor sap Epsilon–he was convinced, so great his need for effective communication, that I meant it just for him. Poor sap me, it turned out that I did.

"If you combine the basic theories of the DNA helix, the fact that we can conceivably restructure genes," he was droning on, with the idea behind Freudian, Jungian, gestalt, psychosomatic medicine suggesting that there is an interrelationship between the conscious part of the brain and the unconscious, autonomic or physiological section. "We can extrapolate the notion that it is within the realm of possibility, through a process of absolute consciousness, to control our own cellular balances and genetic structures–immortality becomes a conscious process."

There were snores and hoots. Even Psi waggled his toes noisily and despaired of ever filling up the collection basket.

"We are not talking so much about a viable possibility in our lifetime, as a direction," Epsilon went on. "But if you do not accept the hypothesis of psychosomatic medicine–even the AMA sees some point to that–you have all of Freud and modern psychoanalysis to answer to. The very fact of modern medicine suggests the intervention of conscious control into unconscious process. At least, I beseech, keep an open mind."

"Okay," he said, thinking now he could give a little teasy bit and wake them up again. "We all know Du Wop has suffered breast cancer. Radical mastectomy; no problem. She's cured. She has written a treatise refuting my theory. Don't worry–we're still friends. Du Wop, however, is fucking up the movement with thwarted love affairs that leave her in irresponsible rages. What do you say we go to work on this."

Now I was indeed intrigued, and looked up at Epsilon in all sincerity.

"Here's what I suggest," he said. "Absolute consciousness at least, to start with, of our own responses to our bodies. Du Wop is titless, with a scar. Her femininity, always tenuous, has been maimed. All she can say is, 'bullshit, what do I need with that.' We try a nudie week at a seashore retreat. We all strip down. Du Wop, because she thinks it's not important, goes along. We start calling her, mildly–over strawberries and cream–titsy, flatty, scar-ola, boobs. We jeer her, the way they used to do at recess. I'm not sure myself just how this works. Within a week, she has experienced all the pains and aches and joys and fears of childhood. She has felt them in her bones, quivered and screeched all down her nerves, tears of pain and love have flowed out of every pore. In short, she has learned to sweat in public. She laughs, 'Scar chests are in, this season, girls.' She says, 'I'm getting mine photographed in *Vogue.'* At the end of the week, all lying on the beach, we start to feel her up, slowly, all the cracks–I, more out of brotherly devotion than lust, run my cock across her wound. I get hard. She wants to suck me off. We all have a go. April fool, we say at last, you might have to make it with a girl. Now, I can't say there's any guarantee we'll cure cancer this way."

"Be fun trying," a voice called out, not Du Wop's, for she was locked up in the decision session.

"Be fun trying," Epsilon repeated gently.

All we could hope for with that, would be to convince Du Wop to pay more attention to her body, feel herself up for lumps. This last one, I have it on good authority went quite awhile unnoticed. Regular exams. Any doubts or fears about it, talk to your local women's group, learn body language, lie down on the floor and get a massage. Maybe share with other smart girls the problems of getting felt up at the Roxy by the usual meathead popcorn picker-upper.

Du Wop is missing out on the experiences of her generation–mostly to good effect, but in the long run bad news for a leader, as for a writer. Removes her from the mass and leaves her with no public stance but to mouth-off shocking points of view that have a chance of being right if reasoned soundly, but as slaps in the face of her constituency just get her old boyfriends organizing against her in the press.

"Wait, wait," came a voice from the rear. "I want to warn you. Mine is an old, hoary voice."

Epsilon looked up from his notes, from which vantage point he had been droning. There was a withered sage with crook and tattered caftan, an albatross, the innards removed to save weight and stench, around his neck.

"Who the fuck are you?" Epsilon called out, annoyed that he had been interrupted just as he was thinking up a decent, mind-boggling conclusion.

"Medicare," groaned the old man. "I have a right to be here. I get in half price. Feds pick up the tab."

"Speak your piece," said Epsilon. "We must get on."

"I am just returned," said the sere and croaky

voice, "from lab experiments performed at Yale Med School on a controlled cohort of college sophomores from around the country. Doing just the sort of thing you say, on just that theory. Only they started on the principle of derangement. Shredded old incendiary pamphlets and term papers, force-fed the resultant verbal codes directly up the assholes and into the intestinal systems of a select group of leadership-quality fraternity brothers and young women who had integrated their beer halls with them. The point was to make a direct neuron link, by bypassing Freud's super-ego, to the local synapse points of the Jungian collective unconscious and thereby humanize the world...You know what? You want to know what? The leader, mind, well, not the leader, just most popular candidate for president of the fraternity, no less came down with a rare muscle disease that turned his entire body from the neck down into a useless sponge."

"I object," said Epsilon. "I object. No more than could be predicted by chance. Check with the AMA. Read–I heartily recommend–Wop's little treatise denouncing me."

"I only warn," the old man cautioned, a crooked finger held aloft. The fury in his rheumy eyes burned fierce. "I only warn. There are more things on heaven and earth than are dreamt of in your philosophy."

"Hey, I'll buy that," said Epsilon. "That's all I ever meant."

With that, we all dispersed. Even Rho zipped up, and, with his collection loot, Psi surreptitiously snuck us Diet Cokes.

5

For me, maybe for all of us, I don't know, I wanted to talk about it with Epsilon, but didn't have the nerve, the turning point came, the gall at the back of the throat, with the question of the investigation into Psi's headstanding proclivities.

Nobody knew just how Psi had started doing headstands. Psi himself was foggy on the question. When some babies were pushing with their feet against their mothers' laps in an impatience to be standing up and walking, still too young for that, Psi was pushing with his hands. Did he think the human race was backward, or should we say, upside down, not knowing which end to have a leg to stand on? When most children were creeping through their stage for that, Psi was stretching out his arms, anxious to walk that way. His back legs (he was in a four-footed position at the time), his legs, that is to say, failed to rubberize their joints at the proper sequence but his elbows knocked two knees out the other end. He stretched his arms. He learned first to bend over double, rest on his hands and peer through the legs, as most children do, for peekaboo, I see upside down. Then he just stayed that way and stayed that way, stretching and straining to get his legs up over. Did his sense of gravity switch about for being so contorted? Cups caught on tables seem to stand suspended in the air that grew too thick to breathe in right side up. When he was three years old he executed his first handstand, completely on one arm. Doctors were amazed. I thought the fluid in his joints would be much too thin, ichorish, I suppose, for that. One time he showed up pictures of his sixth birthday party with a pin-the-tail-on-the-donkey upside down just for him. All other children had to bend way down blindfolded, but Psi walked over hand over hand then reached up with one hand, but he stuck a little low and hit him on the nose. Immortalized in snapshots for ever after. At seventeen he was good at soccer because his hands were out of the way, anyway. At crucial moments he effected an overhead pass by not only headstands but virtually catching the ball on his feet and throwing it, as it were, feet on over the goal. For girlfriends he dated there was upside down fucking, which no one much objected to.

HEADSTANDS WILL NOT BE UNDERSTOOD BY THE WORKING CLASS, came the edict from the new Commune Control Community delegation. We had never had that problem before. The tomato Utopians were satisfied to watch Psi do his headstands at the before-mentioned recruitment drives. And it worked, too, to some success. Psi, dressed up in bright red like a tomato, juggled seven tomatoes with his feet and three more with one hand involved, threw in a basil plant or two to make it more difficult to catch. For a demonstration when we took over the canning factory, he showed how the assembly line could be personned by headstands end over end with somersaults along the line, popping tomatoes in the pot with every turn, dazzling us all with show of sequin-covered waggle, taggle in the air and dipsy-doodle on the noodle. At fourteen, he had developed acne between his toes, his body was so confused. A condition too delicate to mention rules out handshakes. He wore the same shoes three years running, for they seldom wore out, so long did he stand upright on his hands. Offered a hand to shake, he waggled toes at the end of a footsore journey across the face of the mother land.

Truly, Psi would not be Psi without his headstands, we protested; surely, the working class can be asked to understand.

To compensate for the manual dexterity lost due to the fact that his hands were so often occupied supporting his body, his toes developed more than usual prehensile adaptability. He could shred lettuce with his two big toes working together. All five toes working on one foot could sew peacock feathers on the leather protectors he wore on the smaller fingers of his hands. He had not only learned to type, but to file, to answer telephones foot end up. Didn't that give him some extra value to the Utopian evolution, we protested?

But hasn't it been shown, time without end, came the answer, that when one person has a trait or a tendency that he wants to stand alone with, it makes it look as if others don't want to come along?

At one time, so much did he want to be understood while standing under, so to speak, that he attenuated the frown lines across his forehead so that, while in his wonted position it looked like a smile across his face. Doesn't that indicate that when one person loves the way he does things without charging more than double for the show, he ought to have a right to count us in on that?

We were told there could be consequences if Psi persisted in wangling his dangling in the face of the new coalition. The CCC or "C^3" paid a visit to Psi's house to talk to distant relatives if any could be found who might know a way to put a stop to his natural functions.

Psi's apartment could be entered in the usual way, and the furniture had not been affixed to the ceiling. Not exactly. Yet it did not exactly stand so neatly on the floor. A footstool was suspended end over end from the ceiling, in a petit point pattern of a scene with dogs hunting, ducks, it was presumed, dangling at just the height for Psi to rest his feet on when fully stretched up to full headstanding height. Another footstool farther up was raised a foot or so in height from the first to accommodate Psi while elevated to maximum height raised upon both hands. There were small padded tables onto which Psi could climb, hand over hand, to raise himself up to the height necessary to change a lightbulb in the ceiling fixture, feet working the various mechanisms required for that. When C^3 came on the scene they found Psi ever so delicately bent over double to reach a toe to flick the stations of his television set. Some of us had had some inkling that the visit might come to pass and sent a few of us over to help along the talk.

"All right, well, in the privacy of your own home, well, nobody of course can object. But it seems to be disturbing to other peoples' children to watch you do a thing when no one can understand why you want to do it."

Psi was not given to answering for himself. He peeled three bananas with his toes and sliced up half a dozen oranges to hand around to the gathered guests.

Epsilon offered to make a speech in Psi's defense, but was told that would make it even worse.

"We're stumped, if you must know," came the C^3's complaint. "We're asking you nicely just this once to stop."

"But Psi gets so dizzy right side up," we said. He tells the dumbest jokes that way.

"Psi can shuck corn faster with his two feet working at top speed than most corn workers shuck them in a week."

"But that's just the point. Nobody can figure out why he does it."

"There's some speculation that he cornered the market in the special multicolored socks he wears with each toe knitted in for full digital usage."

"There's some thought that he lost a girlfriend for pulling the wool over too many peoples' front teeth, and is trying to compensate for the effect. The point is, it can't go on."

"Or else–?"

"There's no place in a world such is being made better for all the people in it for one person to standout with his own device for buttering bread the way he does it with the big toe working so much like a thumb."

"Or else–?"

"Granted, if the evolution is completely successful and we take over more than canneries–wheat, grain, any beans, so on and so forth, a place must be found or where else will he go?"

"But that's just the point we like to make," we said.

"In the meantime, the working class will never understand. Since we live in the era of transition from one form on the way to Utopia, that must count for prime with us. The workers must try to understand but what they can't see we mustn't force past their usual feeding times."

We paused to reconsider how we could be asked to go along.

6

We were all at a loss to know what to do to defend Psi. His art was nothing you could publish in the bourgeois press where the dissidents might read it. His was mostly a private matter. Maxine covered his stunts in arts and crafts with an old Argus C-3, in the hope of joining the next wave of WPA photographers. Her approach to the various angles of Psi's headstanding, in case we could form a committee, was political–"didactic," Epsilon sneered, rather than aesthetic. She did achieve, notwithstanding, a good range of grays, but the purpose was defeated because it served the purpose.

We went, all of us, to appeal to Du Wop, who now had a private office with several flowering plants.

"The vegetarian question is foremost on the agenda," Du Wop said, after listening to our case, smiling with appreciation while Psi did a little dance with rings on his fingers and bells on his toes, and Maxine personned a backdrop slide show of Psi and us in our haunts.

"We cannot divide the attention of our constituency," she went on. "We've reached a united front agreement with the cannery workers; we've discussed several essays by Percy Bysshe Shelley. Children, just as you say, have been consulted. Theirs, in some cases was the deciding vote."

"I don't want to affront you, Du Wop," Epsilon said timidly. "But could you explain it to us?"

"I don't mind explaining, this one time, but you must then go forth and spread the news yourself. Each one teach one. Or you won't get C^3 grants."

Epsilon looked puzzled, but clamped his lips tight shut.

"Shoot," I said, and for a moment I thought she really might.

"We want to build a humanitarian society,"

she said. "Our side voted for it. Cute Shlong and the cannery workers voted for it. Epsilon has some schemes, I understand, about how we all can just live on forever. Hell, then what do we do. Well, the point is that idea can only be undertaken safely in the humanitarian world. First stage, give up eating meat."

"The Shelley," I said.

"You've heard of it."

"Killing beasts brings out the killer instinct in us, makes killers of us in our political and personal worlds as well. We internalize the savagery of hunting when we draw our knives through a piece of meat."

"Not to mention animal experiments."

"We give up on the aphid project?" I asked.

Du Wop paused a moment. I wondered if the grant money flickered through her brain.

"Aphids, really are a lower form of being," she said at last.

"Then we can eat them?" I asked. It came out a baby voice.

"If you must," she said tolerantly.

Much to our surprise, Rho moved Maxine up from off his lap, stood up full, strode up to Du Wop's desk.

"Why were we not asked to vote," he said in a low voice that still sounded like a demand.

Du Wop was stunned.

"Your democracy here is representational," she said. "We represent you. This saves you from having to do your own voting."

"We are yet stuck with our own thinking," said Rho.

"What is your case?

"We are adults," said Rho. "We have the capacity to eat meat or not eat meat as we choose and control our killer instincts consciously. Furthermore, we are the superior species, 'the responsables' of this planet. If we need to eat the chickie and the duckie and the turkey and goosie to stay alive till we can figure out a better way, so be it."

"That's a fascist argument," said Du Wop. "I have nothing more to say about it. You figure it out for yourselves."

"Individual choice," said Maxine. "Didn't anyone figure out how we could preserve individual choice?"

"Defeats the purpose of humanist collectivism," said Du Wop. "And undermines rational, conscious organization. You can't have an anti-meat-eating and a meat-eating economy at the same time."

I opened my mouth. Epsilon, not knowing what he wanted to say, took my hand in his. We all knew instinctively that to persist to go on with it would just jeopardize Psi's position and there'd be no more sideline favoritism from Du Wop.

7

In its infinite wisdom, the Commune Central Committee planned a secret mission, high priority, involving us, which they did not tell us about. All we knew, it would mean taking the Chevy van into town and Epsilon would have to drive. The catch was that Epsilon still did not know how to drive–and we were all too scared to tell the C^3 that we had shirked our duty–in case it was our duty–to teach him. We could get him papers. The class war had heated up enough so that we had license-forging equipment on the premises. There was just a matter of road experience. Epsilon had none. It fell to my lot to take him in hand.

I backed the Chevy van out for him, motioned him into the drivers seat. He fumbled with the brake, lurched a bit on the house road, then smoothed out his stroke within a hundred yards of the back country macadam. I kept my voice soft yet firm, cautioned him not to swing too wide back and forth, a light touch on the wheel, the car would hold the road. Gave him advance warning on the first stop sign, told him when to ease the brake. Guided him a bit the next stop sign, after that he managed on his own. A hairpin curve too fast–he turned pale but didn't speak. All those years of feeling inadequate as a man and saying it didn't matter, letting someone else drive. It was a quiet road, not much traffic, not much chance to practice passing. Nonetheless, I explained the markings as we went, the dotted line, the solids, two solid lines together, told him all. On the very first try–a slow-moving swine hauler with Dubuque plates–Epsilon, without first asking me, made it around where he was allowed and got back in his lane. The confidence gleamed from his eyes. The manhood on him now was a palpable stench (or was that the swine hauler, now receding fast behind us?). He picked up speed. I raised a hand. He steadied on a straightaway and finessed a traffic circle. Cocksure, yet a touch grateful, he turned to me, daring, now, to take his eyes off the straight line down the road.

"How are you going to do it?" he asked.

"Do what?" I said. "More and more of our lives seem to be determined by the CCC. It may not be up to me."

"How are you going to get me into bed?" he said with a broad, self-pleased smirk.

"It takes two," I said noncommittally.

"I know," he said. "But I mean what are you going to do to me? What will you want from me? What are your positions, your fantasies and all?"

I studied the road a minute. Epsilon, I knew, had a remarkable ability to keep his attention fixed on what he was doing while his head lolled back and forth with sex.

"I don't want to say it," I said. "I'm embarrassed. I've only told a few guys. Already I'm known as the Walt Disney of sexual fantasists. I'm afraid my stuff's too clean."

"Clean," said Epsilon. He went to stroke his chin, saw a curve ahead, lowed a bit, clutched back at the wheel. "I can do clean," he said. "I think I'm game for that."

"Okay then, here goes. My sexual style is

founded on the principle of the asymptote in geometry. Analytic geometry and calculus, actually, the mathematical concept that you come as close as you please without touching, ever closer. Actual insertion and mutual orgasm is the limit on the graph as desire and strokes approach infinity. In a word, delay, anticipation, the art of the custom-designed seduction."

"I was a flop fuck at math," said Epsilon, slowing for a yellow light, then, with expertise, gliding right on through before the red.

"You can make it up in bed."

"I never tried asymptotes. As I said. I'm game. How, then, does this work?"

"Imagine we're virgins fixed up by a matchmaker–they say every true love was made in heaven. Give ourselves a month, say six weeks of serious anticipation. Stay in shape with whoever, in the meantime if you must."

Without my even telling him, I noticed Epsilon checked the rear-view mirror and the side. I had forgotten to tell him that.

"Go on," he said.

"On some pretext, I stay after a lecture with you. We go out to eat somewhere near my digs. The first time, you pay, just to do it right. You agree, and this is up to you, to come up to my house."

Epsilon smirked.

"It's that simple."

"Wait," I said. "Just wait. Toad is home. He's fixed himself some dinner. I introduce you. Suggest a game of dominoes. We have a classy set. It's all we have that wasn't confiscated for the child care center off Basil 3. Toad is into dominoes. In case you don't know dominoes, I help you with your hand. I whisper in your ear about the strategy of playing the doubles, how to use your choices to block him, open up for you. Our hands touch; the tops of our things, of course through clothes. Toad wins. Playfully, we curse and congratulate him. I back off and let you two play against each other. Toad wins again of course and I tell you how he used to cheat at Candyland when he was three and knew shortcuts to Uncle Wiggly that none of us could guess. You put your hands on Toad's shoulders and commiserate about mamas who embarrass you with stories of when you were very young. Toad pushes you away suddenly, but just as suddenly, warmly, as only Toad can smile. You sense his physicalness, his capacity to turn amazingly violent–which may be latent in us all–you think you might want him on your side. You smile. We agree to play one full round, three-handed, to a hundred. You do not like my formica table against which the indeed classy, almost ivory inlaid dominoes inlaid rectangles click. I explain the dominoes were a Christmas gift from my Boone folks in Connecticut, who are generous with gifts. You don't seem to care. You're concentrating on the strategies, making up some of your own so it won't look as if I taught you all you know. You win a round but you're too far behind. I win a couple, but Toad wipes us out. Loser buys ice cream, you say. Awkward, we all go out. I eat Jell-O without whipped cream to try to bring down my weight. You see me to the door, kiss my cheek, I yours, shake hands with Toad. He does a playful bit with fists. You go home.

"The next time, after next lecture, I offer you a home-cooked meal–on me–you bring wine. We must have macaroni in tomato basil sauce, or it'll look bad for us. But I also have some asparagus I snuck in among the basil plants. Toad has copped a few slices of veal from the meat-eaters black market in town. There are mushrooms on a hidden windowsill. Garlic is sanctioned to go with tomato basil sauce and arouses no suspicion. However, we dare not use marsala and then have red to drink as that will raise eyebrows–what? meat to go with marsala sauce? So bring white wine and I'll have lemon. We're allowed salad. I have some local custard I make like my grandma used to for my diabetic grandfather, only for yours I'll use real sugar. I was only able to get the milk that had been contaminated by Queen Anne's lace so it may taste rather gassy. I was told all the rest was going to a recruitment drive among macaroni fieldworkers. For this time I will have bought one of those dingbat word games they recommend to teachers. Together, we will laugh at the absurdisms you make when it's your toss while both keeping a discreet eye on Toad to see he gets his sentence structures right. Afterward tinned fruit and coffee. I'm sorry, the fresh strawberries were for revolutions overseas. You will have smuggled me some Grand Marnier because of your privileged position as a seasoned lecturer, and we will park on my couch in front of the TV while Toad goes in his room to practice his new bass riff. You will put your arm around my shoulder, I will move in close and breathe heavily, and we will watch some blathery old movie I can't stand, sipping, between sighs, our liqueur.

"Finally, after a few weeks of that, you will say, I think it's time we tried a little action. I will say–will you trust me? Let me make the plans? You will nod, scared. July Fourth, I'll say. Or maybe Thanksgiving. Something we can remember later and for which we have some time. You will nod again, and say, I'm your man, babe.

"I won't tell you where you're going, only what to pack, until you get in the passenger side of the Chevy van, which I will manage somehow to requisition. Toad will be off-campus with his dad.

"We're going to Hadlyme, Connecticut, to visit my Boone folks, who are sympathetic to the cause but see no need to work for it, for reasons you will see. They're not strict about their moral code, but we can't sleep together at their place unless we're married. You agreed I could put a hotel room on your American Express. The Griswold, a short walk from the river, built 1769. Across the street is the boatyard where they built the *Oliver Cromwell*, first American Revolutionary War ship. Out on the pier, a jazzy seafood place, where, after parking our stuff in a slightly short-ceilinged, plank floored room, we settle down to eat. Shops are charming to walk among even when they're closed for the night, and there are the yachts. Back at the hotel, we take it slow and easy. I've brought the rest of the Grand Marnier. Plus bubble bath. We fit funny together in an old claw-footed tub. Cleaning each other in all the folds as if we were each other's child. Then, stretched across the nubby antique hand-crocheted white spread, taking turns at massage. A little wilder. Toes dipped in Grand Marnier and sucked off. The other parts. Finally settling into the negotiation of positions. I've found sideways sometimes does well for me. You get to choose a few. If I do lose weight, we'll keep the lights turned low. If not, I may try the one about imagine I am pregnant, but do it in the dark.

"Next day, breakfast in the Griswold's Colonial Room. I stick to fruit compote. I think they have some early American version of bangers you might try. The skim milk on hot cereal does not taste like Queen Anne's lace, but may have DDT.

"We have choices, what with the Chevy van–Mystic seaport reconstructed whaling village; my cousin Liz's husband pilots a ferry across the Sound; the beach ten minutes down the highway at Amagasett; the Groton Submarine works, which the Commune Commission may want to know about, and that would enhance our prestige to report on; or a run up to Newport to see the counterrevolutionaries' digs.

"Dinner with the Boones. It's always somebody's birthday. This time, as a surprise, I have brought a set of put-together toys from the Metropolitan Museum of Art that snap together into fanciful sculptures, of your own design. I ask you to sign the card then say you owe me twenty bucks for your half. They will not make a commotion over you; and will seem to hardly acknowledge you. There's always so many, wandering in and out. The house, of their own design and build, is plenty large enough–my uncle, the town doctor by trade, chose his own trees to adze by hand into beams, guyed them into the cathedral ceiling by himself. Just London broil and baked potatoes, frozen peas and salad with bottled dressing. Rolls. But the children like that and there are lots of kids. The care and imagination has gone into the birthday cake. More toys, clothes and well thought out kid crapola in two hours than you and I combined saw on birthdays and Christmases our whole sapkid lives. We are both pleased that Boone Kid[32] likes our gift. Mathers come in with more shit and sit and schmooze a bit. More of them little short guys. We sit down on the floor, thankful to get a cup of coffee, the strongest drink in the house, and put together our sculptures, with the company of one or two silky blond five-year-old girls as pretext. The first one gives us her impression of what we're making and we start to talk. She joins us. We show her how it works. She finds a space. Another blondie with big blue eyes comes over with a book I have given her on a previous occasion. She asks if anyone will read it to her. Without really thinking about it, you volunteer. Mentally, as the girl-child nestles at your side, you critique the imagery, the slowness of the plot. You do not say this aloud. She brings you more. You discover that the new books they have these days are a lot jazzier than that old Secret Garden malarkey they used to foist on us. And more realistic than Oz. You wonder, as you read, if you could try her on Hawthorne. After three books, you both grow weary. Embarrassed, you get up to stretch.

"'Well, Ep,' I say, 'we can either wash dishes or play pool. We do a bit of both.' You like to show, in these circumstances, that you're not a bigot. But you much prefer pool. Upstairs, in the playroom, not paneled yet, so the insulation shows. Cousin Ken-in-law has come along with his new three-month daughter asleep on his shoulder. You wonder how he works it, are surprised when, when it's his turn to shoot, he hands the kid to you, placing her warm damp body with the little booties on your shoulder so that only your turtleneck separates you from her heat. You stand stiff as a ramrod, your arm getting numb, and hope she doesn't pee. I scratch a couple of times, bank a long one. I'm not really good at this. Learned to be fair enough to keep up with my boys. Cousin Glenn walks in and teases me. He won't tease you. Doesn't know you well enough. He takes a shot. Oh, yes, the baby–we're passing her back and forth now, not all the time to me. She never wakes up, just sucks her thumb and drools, the sweat of the hot night making little ringlets in her hair pressed into everybody's shoulder. Glenn says he's building a little house for sale on Pop and Mom's plot closer to the shore–he's a beginning contractor, I explain. Did we want to drive out tomorrow and take a look, he says. I look at you. Ken-in-law is holding his own little girl so both of us are free to shrug and check it out. I don't really think so, you say. Rain check. I have to get back early tomorrow. Commune business to attend to.

"My cousin Liz comes in, gorgeous in her

vibrancy without makeup and lasciviously tendrilled mane. She's wearing shorts and a tight tee, plumpish, but with a waist, that I don't have–yet. She's my favorite girl–here. The baby wakes up, cries and spits, and we have to stop the play to wait for Ken-in-law to take her down to mommy for a nurse. Meanwhile, I see you appraising Liz; she seems to like you, too. I smile a secret smile. I will get you this evening, I think. Make you imagine a menage. Now, with a bit of sexual appetite awakened in the room, we all set to play a fast, fierce competitive game of eight-ball, which Glenn, for all his girth, wins. You want to play another. Liz's tit has brushed your arm. One of the little girls has come up dressed just in underpants and is picking up the balls that drop out of the broken pocket. Liz has arched her back, stretching the length of her cue stick, showing off truly wonderful breasts. And god, you can't but help know she knows it and know she's doing it for you. I smile to myself again. You and Liz are in fierce competition to get your balls out without dropping in the eight. She even has a sexy way of chalking up the cue. What you don't know is that I know all that, too. In the middle of the game, maddening you, I ask Liz how her photography project is going. You are trying to concentrate on the last one, at last, the eight. If you don't get it, Liz will, she's that good. You want to show her you can win. She's talking to me about double images and time elements and the subtle changes you can catch in multiple exposures. I am urging her on. She no longer cares about beating you. You get the eight ball in, but Liz and I are engaged in a discussion of Margaret Bourke-White. You have to announce to us that you have won. Almost making fun, we both applaud. You feel like an ass. Epsilon knows quite a bit about photography and video and film, I say. Oh? Liz says. You hate yourself for feeling gratified that she looks up. What do you say, she says, stretching, once again, that magnificent chest, we all jump in the pool and talk about it there. It's too damn hot up here. And that is what we do.

"The pool is a hotbed of eroticism, it turns out. Just Liz and you and I at first. Overhead' spots on. Half moon. Little blinky lights beyond the river. Chirrup of crickets in the night-blooming myrtle; fireflies along the hedges to keep untended toddlers out. Liz gets us going on three-person races, which, of course, she wins, but you come close. In between she calls out, You're really into film? You gulp for air, feel the chlorine in your nose, can't do this like you used to but you don't tell her. A light at the bottom of the diving board shows how gracefully her legs move. I used to make a film or two, you gasp. The two oldest grandchildren come out, one in late teens, a girl, the other a thoughtful, pudgy boy. It's hot over in Deep River, Mom let us come on over here, the girl calls out. Gets in the pool in a two-piece red job that shows the bloom of boobs. She swims two laps before she stops so I can introduce you to her and her sensitive kid brother. They turn away, but the girl looks back; Linda, her name is, then, shyly, smiles.

"'Damn,' I says to myself, 'he still looks good. I may get this till he's ninety.'

"'What do you say to volleyball,' Liz calls out. You make a puzzled frown. 'Come on,' she calls. 'Help me with the net.'

"We all set it up across the pool, hunt up the outsize rubber ball.

"'How about Epsilon on my side,' Liz calls to me over the splash of jumping in the pool. I consider a moment. We're determining your fate, she and I, I think. I can tell from her tone of voice. She wants me to decide.

"'Sure, hell,' I say. 'He's all yours.' I'll take the kids on my team. Roughhousing, splashing, jungle competition. You get more than one feel of leg as it brushes past your balls. It is difficult, with the wavery splashing, to see if you have an erection, difficult even with the cool foam, for you to feel just what your cock is doing; but we both know you haven't felt this young in years.

"My aunt Nancy comes out, stocky in her flap-skirt suit, and slowly, at the shallow end, swims gracefully back and forth. Liz's husband shows up from ferrying his boat across the Sound. He's tired and wants some grub. After the kids and I put away the net and ball, I find you talking to Aunt Nancy, not really all that much older than you. It was hot in the kitchen, she says. But I had to finish up. She's almost apologizing for being here with us, taking up swim space in the pool. We should have helped more, you say. Not at all, she says. I wanted you to have a good time. You look into her face, the dark limpid eyes, imagine her as a Yale art student, eighteen or twenty; god, what a beautiful young woman she must have been. Takes your breath away. She is still standing at the edge of the pool, looking up at you, breathing a bit thickly from the swim. I just wanted to cool off–she apologizes again.

"'I feel like I'm meeting a celebrity, Mrs.

Boone,'" you say.

"'Oh. Nancy.' She laughs softly. 'Of course you must always call me Nancy.' She has missed your cue, you think.

"'How do you mean a celebrity?' she says, when you'd just decided to get you of the water. You flash her your most flirtatious smile, just to make sure it's still in working order.

"'Co-producer to this spread,' you say.

"'Oh, it's Len, my husband' she says. But there is a flash in her eyes. She has caught your look. Answers in her way, 'Len did all the work. I was busy with the kids.'

"To get away from the cloying goodness of this household where you can say no curse but durn or pshaw, to get ourselves back in the mood, we run the van down to the Deep River Road House, where Artie Boone, the youngest, plays the synthesizer while Sal, his gal, tends bar. You order, though you don't like to drink, a double Dewar's on the rocks. I stick to seltzer, for my weight.

"'Sal is a bit of a writer,' I say. 'Took some courses up at U Conn.'

"Sal's a pretty girl, older than Artie, with long straight blond hair in a classy Mary Travers cut. You like the dimple in her chin. Sit down, you say to her.

"I lecture, from time to time on problems of writers. I think I know something of that,' you say.

"'Well, I don't have anything to show,' she says. 'Just one little story I've been trying for years to polish right.'

"'That's all right,' you say, 'I'd like to see it. You must learn a lot about people in a place like this.'

"She looks around.

"'I guess I have a minute, till Artie finishes his set.'

"Sits down. A black guy I've met here before comes by and reaches out a hand without a word, knowing I'll take it, as I do, and I get up and dance. You seem not to notice. I come back when the set is finished and Sal's gone. You ordered a seltzer chaser for the scotch. Without asking, I sip from your glass. You look at me sternly. I nurse the glass a bit then smile, in my funny secret way. You decide it is, god help you, a damned charming little smile. You urge me to come away.

"Back at the Griswold, no baths, no massage. Sexed up from womanizing, however mildly, furious at me for interrupting your best flirts, you almost tear my clothes off. I do the same, for my part, unto you. There follows five hours' worth of what is known on my turf as serious, heavy-duty, industrial-strength fornication. We're talking inside out and upside down five hours straight. Stopping to wipe off sweat and to suck it up again. God, like you haven't done since you were seventeen.

"Afterward, spent, we lie back together, sipping water from hotel glasses, though the ice is mostly gone, wishing in an idle way, that we hadn't some years back given up smoking.

"'If we do get married,' you say, 'and that's by no means decided–just a whim that ran through my head.'

"'Okay,' I say. 'It's really okay.'

"'Well, if we do,' you say. 'I want to do it in a church. Just the smallest possible ceremony, your folks and kids, my closest friends, maybe party afterwards at your place. My mother would have liked that. She's gone now, but even genetically speaking, she lives on with me. I'll look at all the flowers, the priests, your pretty eyes. I'll imagine that she's there.'

"I take your hand.

"'I always, at times like these,' I say, 'remember the Lord's prayer.'

"'Our Father...,' you begin.

"'Mother,' I correct.

"You play-punch me upside my head.

'"Hallowed be thy name. They kingdom come'

"We are reciting it now, hand in hand, together.

'"Thy will be done. On Earth as it is in Heaven.'

"We are silent now. I do not tell you that that prayer always makes me weep. You pull your hand away from mine, fold your arms across your chest.

"'Damn,' you say. 'Sure wish I had a smoke. Thirteen years later, I'm still going cold turkey.'

"'We sleep late in the morning, breakfast, then head back. I insist that you drive. We are silent awhile, once we're settled in the van, then open up and talk.'"

"Hey," said Epsilon, "as we came off the back roads, the highway's up ahead. Now what do I do?"

"Get on," I said, "It's the route we're supposed to be checking out."

"But," said Epsilon, "I mean, hell, they drive very fast."

"You'll have to speed up, too. But stay in the slow lane–on the lane–on the right. Just watch out–they'll merge on you. Remember your mirrors and don't trust them. You need to turn your head around real quick to cover the blind spot and not lose track of what's ahead. That's the only hard part. As my grandma Boone used to say: *This is the story of Jonathan Gray, who died defending his right of way. He was right, dead right, as he drove along, but he's just as dead as if he were wrong."*

"What's that mean?" said Epsilon.

"This is not the time or the place to fight for your rights," I said.

"That's not my style, anyway," Epsilon said.

"I know too well."

He frowned.

"What I mean is, you're a sensitive guy, not a pushy type. You need to use that a little better. Get into someone else's reality. Anticipate your opposition. The other driver. Psych out what they're doing before they do it, know what you have to do, to respond before you have to respond, before you have to know. You draw on your own self-awareness, then project it. Learn to observe closely the styles, the patterns, of the guy in front of you, behind you, on either side. Never, never, never, get into fights with trucks, buses, or cops. On the road, outrage is a useless commodity."

"What highway are we on?" Epsilon asked. "I don't see any sign."

"U.S. 69," I said, "try to keep track where you are. You won't see any signs on this road. The kids always steal them for their rooms."

Epsilon laughed and, turning away from me, entered the merge line.

"My grandma had another one she made us learn by heart," I said. I paused. "Wanna hear? *I hate to go above you, I whispered low, because, you see, I love you."*

"Shut up," said Epsilon, "can't you see I have to drive?"

8

So I said
take the ten million dollars,
and to hell with the communist party.

—Anonymous

To make things run smoother, and get the cannery workers integrated in better with the old-line tomato-basil collectivists, the C^3 instituted criticism/self-criticism sessions during lunch breaks and coffee stops in both field and shop. Whichever stint you had, there was no avoiding them. All of us by that time were too tired to even think of raising the question of having a vote on this, or discussing it among ourselves. As it happened, the "C/SC" sessions began harmlessly enough. The point was to discover what unconscious forces were at work on each member that impeded functioning at the task. Childhood would be explored. Sexual proclivity.

When it was discovered that Rho had difficulty getting out the last puff of air during the crucial stage of sealing jars steaming with fresh-packed tomatoes, basil showing through, we all went to work. Several sessions of intensive free association brought us no leads. Finally, near the bell that would call us back to our respective callings, Rho blurted out,

"I'm sorry. I've been holding back. There is something. I have never, that is...this is hard to say. I have never actually ejaculated, really got off, shot my wad into a woman's vagina."

We gasped and sighed and hung out a bit after the bell for consoling pats, and there, theres.

Over the next several weeks, meeting every day, we resolved to set Rho straight. Our foreman, also not elected, saw in this the possibility of making a gestalt for Rho so that he could, once cured of the primary sexual dysfunction, learn to get his bottles sealed, the last whoosh of air shot out.

Rho wasn't a handsome man, but he was still youngish and had an endearing smile, a good physique. He worked out regularly in the collective's gym, pious, devout, worshiped, complete with rosary, the humanistic ideal, played basketball with the younger boys, as sort of free-lance coach. His father had abandoned the family when he was six, and he had been placed in the village orphanage, raised by priests. Later, found the switch to the humanist faith easy enough to make.

"Rage," Maxine suggested. She felt cheated. All these months of tenderly nursing his erections, no payoff. Still felt enough affection to hope it worked out so that they might really get it off.

"What do you mean, 'rage'?" Epsilon said.

"He's angry at his father," said Du Wop. "He needs to get it out. Just let the rage pour forth, sure as spurting his hot sperm."

We all brought in a pillow. Epsilon sat back and watched. But even given a pillow to pound, Rho could find no curses, no threats, no primal scream to direct against his folks.

"Let me try that," Epsilon said. "Let me show you how. Just, you know, to help." He got down on his hands and knees and pounded the pillow for all he was worth.

"Hashslinger," he called out. "Tart-chaser. Leave me, will you. Just with Mama. Strip poker. Night on night."

He tried a primal scream. Usually had good control over his utterances. Could force himself to say what he didn't necessarily mean. This, this rage, he felt.

"Commie, commie, dirty red," he got out.

"Meathead. Twerp. Buffoon." Then there was a series of high, strained 'aiiyees.' At last, his throat raw, the words spent, he remembered Melinda Sweetwater, fell on the floor and wept. When he got up there wasn't a dry eye in the house. I went through several knots of linen handkerchief myself. Rho marveled. Wiping himself off, Epsilon discovered his pants were wet with cum. He could not quite find a way to point this out to Rho.

"You did that very well," said Rho. "I think it really helped me.

"I try to give you your money's worth." said Epsilon, "What the hell–the fee is sixteen ninety-five. I just get ten percent."

What finally got poor Rho was when Maxine attacked his mother.

"She sure left you a wretch," said Maxine. "Blubbery sorry for yourself, when the sun is shining and the surf is up. What do you have a body for if not to dunk it in the foam? Don't you know the motto of the C/SC is: IF YOU KEEP YOUR HEAD STUCK UP YOUR OWN ASSHOLE, OF COURSE THE WORLD WILL STINK LIKE SHIT."

Well, that settled it. Piqued at being, not for the first time in his life, called namby pamby mama's boy, Rho hauled off and popped her in the mouth. He had to admit, ejaculation or no, he felt a lot better. She responded with a sharp blow at his ear.

"Why you," he said and shoved an elbow in her ribs. By now they were play-fighting, laughing tears of sweet pain that made them feel their hurts nudging at their joints.

"Fuck you, motherfucker, in the words of the modern bards," shouted Maxine gleefully.

Rho threw the pillow at her face. This caught on. There were, happily, enough pillows to go around and with shouts of 'fuckyoumotherfucker' on every lip we chucked them all about. Epsilon clipped me a buttoned one square on the jaw. I knew he had a weak spine. I wrestled him to the ground.

"Come in a crack, you break your mother's back," I hooted, "but for only him to hear."

"You are a witch," he said, "a bat right out of hell. The maddest idiot in the village. I want nothing more to do with you."

Then he found an ice cube in a water pitcher and stuffed it in my blouse. So it went at all quarters. Since this was lunch break we all had a chance to get a lot of shit out. When we looked up, Maxine and Rho were sitting in the corner by a pile of shredded pamphlets, beaming pleased as punch, naked to the gills.

"He did it," Maxine breathed. "He shot it all into me. I could even feel its heat."

We all cheered and carried the happy naked couple in a parade up on our shoulders, prancing, pleased with ourselves, till the whistle blew and we had to hightail it back to the production line.

When it ws found the C/SC sessions paid off–Rho did indeed get that last whiff out of each jar as they came through from vacuum pack (for reasons that puzzled me in a way they did no one else), it was decided to take our weekends over for marathon C/SC sessions in order to up the output, since the class war was heating up.

9

The mission, for which Epsilon was not happily prepared to show off his driving, I and Du Wop up in the front riding shotgun, turned out to be more complicated than we thought.

"Turn left at the orphanage," said Du Wop.

She was cryptic. Would not tell us what was going on.

"I have to get gas," Epsilon said.

"Hell," she murmured, bit her lip, "I guess there's time."

I saw it parked in the gas station before Epsilon did. White Mercedes Benz, come in from the capitalist road. Melinda Sweetwater, all gussied up, was struggling with the self-service pump. Her hair was dyed bright red, she was dressed in brilliant white. Her sandals had thin straps and heels.

We all heard her curse as she wrestled with the nozzle.

"Don't they have anybody to help?" moaned Epsilon.

I looked at him, at the strange wince on his face, thought of myself.

"Go on," I said, "by now you should know how." Epsilon got out, a bit fumbly, but mostly gracefully, rescued his beloved from the taint of gasoline.

When he was through, listening all the while to her pleasant stream of charm and vitriol about the tough life when there's no service, he looked into her eyes, jade green and charismatic as always. She took out her purse.

"Do I tip you?"

Epsilon didn't even get insulted.

"Old friend," he said. "This is the sort of thing I do for free."

"What are you doing here?" she asked.

"I can't tell you," he said, "but I drove."

She looked over at our Chevy van, smiled condescendingly.

"Those? In that?"

"I've been driving quite a lot," he said, "all kinds of roads. And you?

"Meeting a friend in the village. Don't want them back at home to know. You won't say you saw me?"

His sweetheart's infidelity–even to the husband she had left him for, pained Epsilon. He tried to take to take her hand. She kissed him on the cheek. He could almost remember the name of that perfume. It would come to him.

Back at the car, Du Wop drummed her fingers at the dash.

"I have to meet Cute Shlong, if you must know. We're hooking up with the factory that produces the jars and lids we need at the cannery for the tomato-basil sauce. There are some hotheads among them. The police are on their tail. Cute Shlong is trying to cool them down. I don't know if he can hold out. We will all, each in our own ways, have to help."

"Seems to me you could have told us before you commandeered us," I said. "Any violence?"

"Stay out of the center."

"I've been an outfielder all my life."

The street was quiet when we entered.

Collective stores and co-ops all were closed. The orphanage, at the edge of town seemed the safest spot for us. But we were wrong. We had our eye on an army camouflage truck coming in one direction, an open van of college kids in beards and radical mufti in another. We watched them approach each other. Du Wop, fearless in the teeth of fray, got out. She had a rendez-vous in the orphanage. But she never got that far. There was firing on the road a ahead. Psi, Epsilon and I got out. Because his position, Psi was best in line to jump Du Wop and pull her to the stoop for safety, keep her out of the line of fire. Too close, too close, we heard a huge explosion. It was closer than we thought. The orphanage. Smoke and flames came shooting out. From an upstairs window a mysterious elderly black woman stuck her arms out with a white bundle in two hands.

"Catch, boss man," she called out.

Startled, Epsilon looked up. Without his really knowing how he did it, when he looked down there was a red-faced newborn squaling in his arms.

"Hey, you," the black woman called.

Du Wop was up by now, could see it was hopeless to proceed ahead.

"Yes, you. You are a woman, ain't you? See if you can catch a baby girl."

"Hell," Du Wop called back, "even without a mitt!"

Psi unaccountably stood upright in time to help her make the catch. Similarly, there was one for Maxine and Rho. Epsilon handed me the child, a boy one, I ascertained, and snuck across a line of bullets, belly flopping low to break into the collective store and liberate three huge boxes of paper diapers and some bottles and some milk. Packed in, we squeezed our bundles on our laps and made off.

"Where to?" said Du Wop.

We were surprised. To hear her hesitate and ask us. We stopped at the gas station to get directions to places we might not already know.

"Capitalist Road is bombed out," the grease monkey said. "There's a crossroads up ahead. You might give that a look."

The crossroads turned out to be under repair. New signposts, affixed by the Marx and Engels Construction Company. *Socialism to the east. Barbarism to the west. Dead end straight ahead.*

Epsilon looked to all of us.

"The east road is back to the commune," he

said.

Du Wop was filling a bottle of milk with Similac and for once kept her fool mouth shut and let the rest of us decide. It wasn't fair to overrule her, but just this once we felt we had it coming.

"Eve?" Epsilon turned to me, "How about you?"

"I'm with you, Epsilon, I said, "whither thou wilt go."

We all sat still a minute, unable to decide. A car came up behind us, sure where it was headed. A white Mercedes Benz, with a well-coiffed red-head at the side. And who was that in with her, Du Wop wanted to know. Hell, it was Cute Shlong, cocky, headstrong, blond and freckled, at the steering wheel. They turned, without hesitation, to the east, toward the communes.

Epsilon looked puzzled, and for a moment, hurt.

"Socialism, looks like," I said, "is triumphing with liberty, as the song goes. There's always those that likes triumphant liberators."

I thought Epsilon might slug me, or at least make that terrifying frown. But no, he got out of the car, and bade me come along and bring the babe. The west road led to an open meadow glade where a little brook ran through. Wildflowers and lemon grass grew up in the stretches between trees.

"Know anything about log cabins?" Epsilon said.

"It's been awhile," I said, "I've done that before. Wild berries. I know which ones are good. Milkwood pods, if you boil them, taste like okra. I know more. We can fashion sticks to fish with."

"It's like crash landing on a fucking foreign planet, when you think about it," he said.

"It's reinhabiting our own," I answered.

"Shut up a minute, Eve," he said. "You talk too much, and I think our child has peed."

But I didn't move to change him. Epsilon looked down at me, breathed softly in my ear.

"Eve."

He nuzzled soft short cut wisps of hair.

"Eve, you is my woman now," he said, and then, moving in as close as the babe would allow, thrusting tongues deep in each other's throats, we kissed.

ABOUT THE AUTHOR

Nora Ruth Roberts is the author of over 30 stories, poems and articles, including *Three Radical Women Writers* (Garland, 1996). She is a Contributing Writer to *The Encyclopedia of the American Left* (Oxford) and is a professor at the City University of New York.

Her poetry collection is scheduled to be published currently with Missing Spoke Press. Dr. Roberts holds a Ph.D. in Literature from the City University of New York.